W9-CDO-810

THE CURSE OF THE CAT-EYE JEWEL

THE CURSE OF THE CAT-EYE JEWEL

By Tracey West

Random House 🏠 New York

Manufactured under licence granted to AMEET Sp. z o.o. by the LEGO Group.

AMEET Sp. z o.o.
Nowe Sady 6, 94-102 Łódź—Poland
ameet@ameet.eu
www.ameet.eu

www.LEGO.com

Published in the United States by Random House Children's Books, a division of Penguin Random House LLC, 1745 Broadway, New York, NY 10019, and in Canada by Penguin Random House Canada Limited, Toronto. Random House and the colophon are registered trademarks of Penguin Random House LLC.

rhcbooks.com

ISBN 978-0-593-38140-3 (trade) — ISBN 978-0-593-38141-0 (lib. bdg.)
ISBN 978-0-593-38142-7 (ebook)

Printed in the United States of America

10 9 8 7 6 5 4 3 2 1

First Edition 2021

CONTENTS

◆◆ Prologue ◆◆

Splash!

The Green Ninja backflipped over Kai's head and landed in a puddle. The water shot up and drenched Kai.

"Hey, watch it!" complained Kai, the Fire Ninja. "Master Wu, why do we have to train in the rain?"

Master Wu stood on a rock and watched Lloyd, Kai, Cole, Nya, and Zane spar with each other outside the Monastery of Spinjitzu. The rain poured down the edges of his round straw hat, leaving his face dry.

"Do you think the weather will obey you when a battle springs up, ninja?" Master Wu asked. "It will not. You must hone your skills in every environment. Do you understand?"

"Yes, Master Wu," Kai grumbled. He leapt in the air and aimed a kick at Cole. Cole dodged it—and slipped in the mud.

"Isn't underground an environment, too?" asked Cole, the Earth Ninja. "Why can't we train there, where it's warm and dry?"

Nya surfed up to the others on a wave of muddy water that she controlled with her elemental power. Each of the ninja had the ability to control the power of an element of nature, and Nya was the Water Ninja.

"I don't see what the problem is," she said. "Training in the rain is fun!"

She jumped off the wave and it sloshed over Lloyd, Cole, Kai, and Zane.

"I agree with Nya," said Zane, the Titanium Ninja. "This reminds me of my early days of training, when I would meditate at the bottom of a lake."

Nya looked around. "Hey, where's Jay? I thought he'd be adding some lightning to this storm."

Jay charged out of the monastery carrying an old-fashioned umbrella with a long bamboo handle and a tiny canopy on top.

"Sorry I'm late!" he said.

"Don't open that!" Master Wu warned.

Jay frowned. "You mean this? I found it in a closet. I figured since it's raining . . ."

"You figured you would train with an umbrella?" Nya asked.

"Why not?" Jay replied. "I can train with one arm and hold the umbrella with the other." He karate-chopped with his left arm to make his point.

"That umbrella is very dangerous, Jay," Master Wu said.

"It's just an umbrella," Jay countered. "What are you worried about? That I'll poke my eye out or something?"

He twirled the umbrella like a baton. The long handle poked him in the eye.

"Ow!" Jay cried.

Master Wu swiftly jumped off his rock and took the umbrella from Jay before he could blink. By now, the

other ninja had gathered around, curious.

"All right, uncle, what's the deal with this umbrella?" Lloyd asked. "There must be a story behind this."

"There is indeed," Master Wu replied. "And since this training exercise seems to be going nowhere, I will tell you. Come inside."

A few minutes later, the ninja were wearing dry clothes and gathered in Master Wu's room. He sat on the floor with the umbrella at his feet.

"Many years ago, when my brother, Garmadon, and I were young, our father sent us on a journey," he began. "The story of this umbrella is the very first adventure we had. . . ."

Chapter 1
The Journey Begins

You boys are both a disappointment to me. So reckless!

The words of the First Spinjitzu Master had echoed in Wu's mind all night. He and his brother, Garmadon, had disappointed him before. But now things were different.

As a young boy, Wu had been impatient. He didn't always obey their father, and sometimes broke the rules. It had been Wu's idea to steal the scrolls of Forbidden Spinjitzu. He'd been sure his father would understand. Aspheera, the Serpentine sorceress, had been planning to invade Ninjago, and he had to stop her! But he wasn't strong enough. He needed the secret power in the scrolls to defeat her.

Garmadon had used the scrolls, too, to battle her snake warriors. Together, the brothers had defeated and imprisoned Aspheera. They'd saved Ninjago!

But their father had been angry, and worse, disappointed. He hid the scrolls where they would never be found. Wu worried that his father would never trust him again.

After that, Wu became the responsible one, and his brother started to take more risks. It was Garmadon who had climbed over the wall when they weren't supposed to. And Garmadon who had been bitten by a serpent on the other side of that wall.

Now, several years later, the First Spinjitzu Master still did not trust them. He had been more silent than ever since they had moved to the monastery. But then,

last night, he had given them both a chance to redeem themselves.

"You have both disobeyed me several times. And since Garmadon was bitten, it has become even worse," their father had said. "Something strange happened to you that day, Garmadon, and I fear you are not the same boy you were before."

Garmadon had scowled but said nothing.

"I am sending you on a journey," their father had continued. "A journey to find a special tea plant that may help purify Garmadon of whatever is plaguing him. You will leave tomorrow morning at sunrise."

Wu had been full of questions. "Where will we find this tea plant? And what is so special about it?"

His father had smiled. "The plant grows on the shores of the northern ocean. Once you get there, more answers will be revealed."

"Mysterious as always," Garmadon had muttered under his breath.

"Did you say something, son?" the First Spinjitzu Master had asked.

"Wise words, Father!" Garmadon said out loud.

Thinking about this new mission was keeping Wu awake. *Where will our journey take us? What will we discover there?* he thought. The thought of exploring Ninjago excited him just as much as making things right with his father.

Before the first ray of sunlight peeked over the mountain, before the first bird sang a single note, Wu jumped out of bed. He put on his gi—brown trousers

with a matching lightweight shirt tied in front. He washed his face in the bowl of water on the simple wooden table in the room. Then he ran a comb through his white-blond hair and topped it with his favorite straw hat.

He had gotten his backpack ready for the journey the night before and slipped it on his back. Then he picked up his bamboo fighting staff.

Garmadon was still in bed, snoring. Wu lightly tapped him on the head with his staff.

"Rise and shine, brother! Today our journey begins!"

Garmadon swatted him away. "Knock it off, Wu. I'm still sleeping!"

"Father said we must leave at sunrise," Wu reminded him.

"Yes, but he didn't say *which* sunrise," Garmadon shot back. "Wake me up tomorrow."

He pulled the blanket over his head and started to snore again.

"Are you serious?" Wu complained. "This is an important mission. We've got to start off on the right foot."

Garmadon just kept snoring.

Wu frowned. Then he picked up the water bowl and emptied it on his brother's head.

Garmadon jolted up, sputtering. "Hey, what do you think you're doing?"

Wu laughed. "Looks like you're awake now."

Garmadon climbed out of bed. "Try that again and I'll hit you with my best Spinjitzu move," he snapped.

"Ooh, I'm scared," Wu replied sarcastically. "Come on, get your bag packed so we can get going. The sun is coming up!"

Grumbling, Garmadon started filling his pack.

"Don't forget something to wear when it gets cold at night," Wu said. "And extra socks in case our feet get wet. And you might want to pack some tea. I packed some along with my teapot, but we could use some more."

"I will pack whatever I want to pack," Garmadon said, and Wu knew better than to argue. Getting his brother out of bed was a victory. Starting their journey was the most important thing!

Wu waited patiently for his brother to get ready. The birds were already on their twenty-fifth song when

Garmadon appeared, with his dark hair tied back and his pack on his back.

"What are you waiting for, Wu? Let's go!" Garmadon said.

The two boys stepped out of the monastery.

"Where are we going, again?" Garmadon asked.

"Right now there is only one path in front of us, so let's take it," Wu said, and they headed for the nearest village.

The village was just starting to wake up when they arrived. Chickens pecked at the ground. Children

carried buckets of water from the well. A jolly man sold noodles from a cart.

"Get your breakfast noodles here!" he called out. "Start your day with a belly full of warm noodles!"

Garmadon stopped in front of the cart.

"Come on," Wu urged. "Father said we need to go to the northern ocean. And north is this way." He pointed to a path outside the village.

"Can't we get some noodles?" Garmadon asked. "It makes sense to get some food in our bellies if we're going on a long journey. The food in our packs will only last for so long."

Wu's stomach growled. "I guess that sounds sensible," he admitted.

The boys bought two bowls of noodles and slurped them down.

"That was pretty good," Garmadon said. "Maybe we should look for a dumpling cart."

"I don't get it," Wu said. "It's like you don't even want to go on this trip. What's the problem?"

"The problem is that Father thinks *I'm* the problem," Garmadon snapped. "I don't need some stupid tea to cure me of anything. I'm just fine!"

Wu stared at his brother. Their father was right. Garmadon had been different since the day the boys had been practicing with their wooden katanas and one had gone flying over the garden wall. Garmadon went to bring it back, but a strange snake bit him as he reached for it.

From that day on, it seemed like evil had found its way into Garmadon's heart. Bad moods would come over him suddenly, like storm clouds on a summer day.

And there was a darkness in his eyes that Wu hadn't seen before.

But Wu didn't say those things out loud.

"Father's just angry with us for stealing the scroll," Wu said. "If getting this tea plant will get him off our backs, we should do it."

Garmadon sighed. "Fine."

They took the path heading north and traveled for several days. They journeyed across fields, climbed hills, and crossed rivers. On the fourth day, they came to a dark forest.

Tall trees towered into the sky, blocking out the sun. Peering into the forest, Wu saw a cloudy, gray mist.

"There's a heavy fog in this forest, which is weird. It's not anywhere outside the forest," he said. He looked left and right. "We could easily get lost in there. Maybe we should walk around it."

"That will take too long," Garmadon said, and he walked into the trees.

Wu frowned and reluctantly followed Garmadon. The brothers took a few steps and the ominous fog completely surrounded them.

"It's impossible to see!" Wu exclaimed. "I *knew* we should have gone around it."

"Just keep walking straight," Garmadon said. "I think I see a light up ahead."

Wu looked into the haze. He saw a light, too—two of them. Two red, glowing lights.

"Garmadon, those look like eyes," Wu said.

"That's just your imagination," his brother replied. "It's probably just—"

RRRRRRWwwwwwwwwR!

A beast with glowing eyes and a mouth full of sharp teeth lunged at them!

Chapter 2
The Mysterious Ninja

Wu dove to the left. Garmadon dove to the right. Both boys somersaulted when they hit the ground.

"What is that thing?" Garmadon called out.

The creature roared again, flailing its arms and turning in a circle, trying to locate the boys. It was hard to see anything in the fog, but Wu could make out a hulking shape. Red eyes bulged from a furry face. Its body seemed to be covered with scales. Paws with sharp claws slashed at the air.

"What kind of monster is this?" Wu yelled as the boys rolled away to avoid the monster's reach. Then Wu and Garmadon jumped to their feet.

"I think it's a lizard!" Garmadon replied.

"I think it's a tiger!" Wu shot back. "Or maybe a bear?"

"Whatever it is, it doesn't like us," Garmadon said. "Time for some Spinjitzu!"

"Ninjaaaaa-gooooooo!" the brothers yelled.

They began to quickly spin, becoming tornados of energy. They whirled toward the creepy monster at top speed.

Whack! The monster swatted the ninja with powerful arms, sending the tornados spinning out of control. Both boys crashed into trees.

"This is a powerful adversary," Wu remarked.

"I can't see anything in this fog except for its glowing eyes," Garmadon complained, running over to his brother. "It's not fair!"

The monster roared again. It was now so close, the boys could smell its horrible, hot breath.

"Maybe tiger-lizard-bears eat dirty socks because that's what its breath smells like," Wu complained as the boys jumped out of the way.

"We need a giant bottle of mouthwash!" Garmadon said.

"That's one plan," Wu replied. "Here's another: Let's work together, side by side. We'll attack from the front."

Garmadon nodded. "All right, but it won't be easy fighting when I'm holding my nose!" he joked.

The two boys began to spin again. They zoomed across the forest floor, following the sound of the monster.

Bam!

They slammed into the monster's hard belly. The creature grabbed one brother in each hand and slammed them into the dirt. Then it planted a paw on each ninja and licked its lips as it hungrily eyed them.

Garmadon struggled to free himself from the heavy paw holding him down. "This guy needs to go on a diet!" he complained.

"My hands are pinned beneath me," Wu said. "Maybe we can use our feet to—"

Whooosshhhhhhhhhhhh!

The monster looked away from the boys and sniffed the air. Something dropped from the sky and landed in front of it. Wu craned his neck to look behind him. Through the mist he made out the shape of a tall, slender woman wearing a ninja uniform with a mane of long hair streaming behind her.

She's either a friend of the monster, or the monster's enemy, Wu thought. *I hope she's an enemy!*

The woman struck the monster across the nose with a weapon that looked like a long staff, and it leapt up, freeing Wu and Garmadon. They quickly scrambled to get back up.

The woman jumped as though her feet were on springs and soared straight into the air. She flew over the monster's head and landed gracefully and silently behind it.

Wu's mouth dropped open. Were those cat ears on top of her head?

The woman spun the staff in front of her, and Wu saw it had an umbrella canopy at the end. She was battling with an umbrella!

Then something happened that surprised him even more. Her body began to whirl and she became a tornado of energy!

"She's doing Spinjitzu!" Wu gasped.

"That's impossible!" Garmadon cried.

The woman circled the monster faster

and faster, creating a wind so forceful that it blew Wu and Garmadon back into the trees. Then . . .

Whack! She smacked the monster with her umbrella. The sheer force of the blow sent it flying over the trees.

Yip! Yip! Yip! The boys heard the creature whimper and then run off, crashing through the brush.

The woman stopped spinning. The wind had blown away the fog, and they could see her clearly as she took off the mask covering her nose and mouth. She had pointy cat ears and long whiskers, and her face was covered with gray fur. She stared at them with yellow cat eyes that sparkled with a mix of amusement and something else the boys didn't recognize.

"Thanks for saving us," Wu said. "Who are you?"

The woman didn't answer. Instead, with one quick move, she disappeared into the trees.

Chapter 3

Attack of the Green Warriors

"Who was that?" Garmadon asked excitedly. "Did you see how fast she was?"

Wu nodded. "She was amazing! The way she took care of that monster was spectacular. How did she jump like that, anyway?"

"And she knows Spinjitzu!" Garmadon added. He looked up. "We should go after her and find out why."

They heard a roar in the distance.

"Or we should get out of this creepy forest while we can," Wu suggested. "Before that monster comes back . . . and brings some friends with it."

"You're no fun, you know that?" Garmadon asked, but he didn't argue.

The brothers made their way through the misty forest, watching and listening for signs of any more monsters. About an hour later, they came out of the woods into a field with a bubbling brook running through it. The sun was slowly setting, streaking the sky with red.

"This looks like a good place to make camp," Wu said, looking around. "We can shelter under that persimmon tree over there and clean up in the brook."

"It's still daylight," Garmadon protested. "Shouldn't we keep going? I just want to get that dumb plant and get back home."

"It's a long journey to the northern shore—you know that," Wu reminded him. "We're going to need to rest sometime, and frankly, after that monster fight, I could use a break."

"Fine!" Garmadon said, and he flopped down under the tree. "If you're so excited to camp out, you can make the fire."

"That's not fair," Wu pointed out. "We need to work together."

Garmadon glared at his brother. "Fine," he said. He slowly got up and helped Wu gather some fallen tree branches and dried leaves. Wu took a fire-starting stone from his pack and within a few minutes, the brothers had a fire going a safe distance from the tree, but close enough to keep them warm.

"So what do you think was up with that cat lady back there?" Garmadon asked, sipping the tea that Wu had prepared over the flames. "I mean, first of all, she was like a human, but also a cat. And she knew Spinjitzu!"

Wu nodded. "I know. It's weird. I mean, I know Father hasn't trained too many people in Spinjitzu. And he's never mentioned training a cat."

Garmadon frowned. "We should have gone after her."

"Why?" Wu asked. "You're the one who's anxious to get the plant and head back home."

His brother shrugged. "I don't know. Curious, I guess," he said.

Wu smiled. "What's that old saying? Curiosity killed the cat?" he asked. "I think it's smart that we let her go her own way."

"Maybe," Garmadon said.

"Well, I'm *feline* hungry," Wu joked as he opened his pack. "How about some rice cakes to go with those persimmons we picked?"

"Sure, as long as you don't serve up another cat pun," Garmadon replied.

"Oh, lighten up. I'm just *kitten* around," Wu teased, and his brother groaned.

After they ate, Wu let out a loud yawn. "We should probably take lookout shifts tonight, to make sure there are no monsters around. We could—"

"I call second shift!" Garmadon yelled.

"You can't just call it," Wu argued.

"I just did," Garmadon said, and he leaned back, using his pack as a pillow.

Wu sighed. "Fine. I'll go first."

They took shifts throughout the night and in the morning they ate some breakfast, bathed in the creek, and safely put out the fire. Birds soared in the blue sky overhead.

"Let's go! We're going to make great ground today!" Garmadon said, sprinting ahead of Wu.

"Wait up!" Wu cried. "We need to plan our course."

"What do you mean?" Garmadon asked. "We need to go north. And that's where we're headed."

"Right," Wu said. "So I'm sure you noticed that tall mountain that's in our way?"

"Wait, what?" Garmadon asked, and he looked up. In the distance, a tall, skinny peak rose high into the sky. "Oh, that mountain. No problem. I am sure we can go around it."

"Maybe," Wu said. "I have no idea what terrain we're going to be dealing with. I'm thinking we should look for a village and find out what the best way is to get through. I think I see a road there heading west, and—"

"Wu, I've been doing everything you want this whole trip," Garmadon said angrily. "And I say that we keep heading north. We'll figure it out as we go."

"Did you forget that you're the one who thought we should go through that forest?" Wu asked. Then he sighed. "Whatever. We'll do it your way. Who knows? Maybe we'll find a village along the way."

But they didn't find a village. They walked through more fields, and another forest (monster-free, thankfully) and a swampy area that left them both feeling cold and clammy. That took them to the mountain foothills—a wide expanse of rocky platforms. The boys climbed them like giant steps.

"Going around the mountain will take some time if it's like this," Wu said. "But the mountain is too steep to climb."

"For once, I agree with you," Garmadon said, and they continued to make their way across the rocky terrain.

AAAAHHHHH!

A loud cry made both boys spin around. A dozen warriors ran toward them. They wore green uniforms with the symbol of a jewel emblazoned on the front. Green hoods covered their darkened faces—and were those triangle-shaped ears on top of each hood?

"Who are those bawlers? Are they attacking us or coming to greet us?" Garmadon asked.

"Maybe they're with the cat lady," Wu suggested. He started waving his arms. "Hello! I'm Wu, and this is my brother, Garmadon."

AAAHHHHH!

The warriors stormed closer.

"I guess they're attacking us!" Wu said.

"We're outnumbered!" Garmadon cried.

"This isn't the first time," Wu said. "Let's give it our best shot."

Garmadon nodded. "I'll take six, you take six."

The boys split up. Garmadon leapt to the next rock, and half of the green warriors charged after him. Wu quickly strategized as the other six warriors rushed toward him.

Wu positioned his fighting staff in front of himself.

RRRRHHHHH!

Whack! He batted away the first warrior who reached him.

Whack! The second tumbled down the rocks.

Two more came at him, one on either side, and Wu jumped as high as he could. The warriors collided into each other and then slumped to the ground.

The fifth warrior held a chain with a curved weapon at the end. He swung it at Wu, who caught it on the end of his staff. Then Wu swung the staff, sending the warrior and his weapon flying.

Umph! The sixth warrior tackled Wu at the knees, pushing him onto his back and knocking the staff out of his hands. Wu kicked up as hard as he could and got the green fighter off him. He jumped to his feet, picked up the staff, and planted it on the warrior's chest.

"Who are you, and why are you attacking us?" he asked. "We're just passing through."

The warrior scowled. Before he could answer, another cry rang through the foothills.

AAAAHHHHH!

A second wave of green warriors, this one twice as big as the first, raced toward them. Wu glanced over at his brother. Garmadon had taken care of his six warriors, too, but could they face more?

"Run!" Wu yelled, and this time, his brother agreed. They raced across the rocks with the green warriors in hot pursuit.

The boys were speeding so fast that they didn't notice the cliff up ahead. They both realized too late—and plummeted into a deep ravine!

Chapter 4
Niñeko

Wu's stomach dropped as he fell. He quickly reached out and grabbed onto a rock that jutted out of the ravine wall. His legs dangled beneath him and he dug his fingers into a crevice. From the corner of his eye, he saw his brother grab onto a rock, too.

Garmadon climbed up to join him.

"You okay?" Wu asked him.

Garmadon nodded. "Yeah. I guess that dangerous death-drop snuck up on us."

"It sure did," Wu agreed. Both boys gazed up.

"What now?" Wu asked. "The sides of this ravine are pretty smooth and steep. How are we going to climb up? We're not mountain goats."

"No, but we're ninja," Garmadon said. "Maybe we could do it if we tried."

"We could climb down," Wu suggested, and when he looked below, he got a little dizzy. "It's a long way, though."

"Up here!" a female voice called out.

Their heads snapped up. The cat ninja gazed down at them, holding her umbrella.

"Jump up and grab it," she instructed.

"I'll go first," Garmadon offered. He leapt up, grabbed the handle of the umbrella, and then propelled himself into a somersault. He landed safely at the top of the ravine.

Wu took a deep breath, let go, and jumped up. He grabbed onto the umbrella, swung up, somersaulted in the air, and . . .

Bam! Slammed right into his brother. The two boys ended up in a tangled heap.

"Watch it, Wu!" Garmadon complained.

"*Me*, watch it? You were in my way!" Wu shot back.

The cat ninja began to laugh, a sound that was somewhere between a human's chuckle and a cat's throaty purr.

"What's so funny?" Garmadon asked.

"I am laughing because when I first spotted you in the forest, I thought I was dealing with two Spinjitzu masters," she replied. "But you appear to be two very silly boys."

"We *are* Spinjitzu masters," Garmadon shot back.

"What my brother means is that we are training to be Spinjitzu masters," Wu said, and he bowed respectfully. "Thanks for saving us. Twice. My name's Wu, and this is Garmadon."

"You're welcome," the cat ninja replied. "I am Nineko."

Wu suddenly realized something. "Where did all those warriors in green go?"

Nineko laughed again. "Warriors? They are merely thugs. They left when they realized you were no threat to them," she said. "And now I must go as well."

"Wait!" Garmadon cried before she could turn around. "We noticed back in the forest that you had some pretty unusual Spinjitzu moves. Maybe you could teach us a few?"

Her mouth twitched. "I would be wasting my time," she said. "It would take years of practice for you to learn my ways."

"But we've had lots of practice," Garmadon said. "Besides, it's in our blood. Our father is the First Spinjitzu Master."

Nineko raised an eyebrow. "Then we have something in common," she said. "For it was your father who trained me."

Wu frowned. "Father never mentioned training a . . ."

"A cat?" she asked, and her yellow eyes gleamed. "No matter. I can see you two will be useful to me. Come."

She turned quickly and began to walk away, carrying her long-handled umbrella.

"Wait, where are we going?" Garmadon asked.

"Come or do not come," Nineko called behind her. "It is your choice."

The brothers looked at each other. Wu frowned. "Curiosity . . . ," he began.

". . . is killing *me*!" Garmadon finished, and he took off after Nineko. Wu shrugged and followed. He had to admit—he was pretty curious, too.

Nineko moved swiftly and silently away from the mountain, back to the swampy area they had passed through earlier. They followed her into a tangle of green plants. Wu hacked at the branches with his staff, and Garmadon sliced through them with his katana. But Nineko weaved through them with no trouble at all.

They emerged from the thicket onto the shores of a lake. Wide green lily pads floated on the calm, deep green surface of the water. Nineko pushed a canoe into the lake and then gracefully stepped into it.

Wu and Garmadon followed her, and they each picked up an oar without being told to. They rowed across the smooth lake, and neither one of them spoke. They could sense that Nineko wouldn't be pleased.

On the opposite shore, a small house stood on stilts as tall as trees. The house was a simple structure with a peaked roof and a wrap around deck.

When they reached the shore, Nineko hopped out of the canoe and nimbly climbed up the ladder to the house. Garmadon and Wu scrambled up behind her. They removed their shoes on the deck and followed her inside.

It appeared to be Nineko's home, and it was simple and clean, with cushions on the floor, a wooden table,

a cabinet, and a sleeping mat. Wood burned in a small metal stove, taking the swampy chill out of the air.

"Excuse me for a moment," Nineko said, and she disappeared through a doorway. A few minutes later she returned, wearing a pale green kimono with a pattern of blue fish printed on it.

"I will make tea," Nineko said, and she removed a clay jar and some cups from the cabinet.

"Thank you," Wu said. "It's kind of you to invite us here. Especially since you knew our father. I have so many questions."

"You may ask them," Nineko said. "But I cannot promise that I will have answers."

"How did you meet our father?" Wu asked.

"I met him many years ago, when I was a girl—a little younger than you," she said.

"A girl—not a cat?" Garmadon asked.

"No, not yet a cat," she said, and Wu heard a hint of sadness in her voice. "He saw potential in me and taught me the basics of Spinjitzu. Then, after . . . after I left him, I created new moves. I call my form of fighting the art of Catjitzu."

"Catjitzu," both boys repeated.

"But why did you leave our father?" Wu asked.

"That does not matter," Nineko replied, and she placed two steaming cups of tea in front of them. "What matters is that you want me to teach you my moves, and I will—if you do me a favor in return."

"Yes!" Garmadon agreed quickly, but at the same time, Wu said, "It depends on the favor."

Nineko sat on a cushion, and a faraway look crossed her eyes. "I seek the Cat-Eye Jewel," she said. "It rightfully belongs to me and those thugs that you call warriors stole it from me."

"About those guys—why do they wear hoods with ears? Are they cat ninja, like you?" Garmadon asked.

"That is not important," she replied. "What's important is that I want the jewel back and I need your help."

Wu thought about this "You have amazing ninja skills," he said. "Why can't *you* steal it?"

"They have put a magical protection around the jewel that prevents cats from getting close to it," Nineko replied. "But if I train you two properly, you should be able to easily steal it for me. Do you agree to our bargain?"

"Our father has sent us on a journey," Wu said. "I'm not sure if we . . ."

"The experiences you have on a journey are often more important than the destination," Garmadon said. "Isn't that what Father always says? Think how impressed he'll be if we come home with some awesome new skills besides that plant he asked for."

Wu considered it. Impressing their father wasn't an easy thing to do. Maybe Garmadon had a point. *And I want to learn Nineko's moves as much as my brother does,* he thought.

"All right," Wu said. "Count us in!"

Chapter 5
The Art of Catjitzu

Nineko yawned.

"I must nap," she said. "We'll train after moonrise."

"Wait!" Wu cried. "Can't you tell us more about your training with our father?"

"And who were those green ninja with the cat ears?" Garmadon asked.

"And what is the Cat-Eye Jewel, and why did they steal it from you?" Wu added.

Nineko shooed them away with a wave of her paws. "Leave me."

Wu and Garmadon left the house and climbed down the ladder. Away from the warmth of the fire, the air felt cold and damp.

"What are we supposed to do here while we wait?" Garmadon complained. "Stare at a stinky lake? And what kind of ninja takes a nap?"

"A cat ninja," Wu replied. "Haven't you ever heard of a catnap? Besides, I think cats are mostly awake at night, anyway."

"But she's not a cat," Garmadon said thoughtfully. "I mean, not *just* a cat. She's part human, too. She said she was a human girl when Father trained her. So how did she become a cat-human?"

"It's all kind of strange," Wu admitted. "But she saved us—twice."

Garmadon nodded. "Yeah, we'd either be monster chow or flat as pancakes right now without her. She's awesome!"

The boys were silent for a while after that. Garmadon tried skipping stones on the surface of the green lake, but the water pulled them beneath the surface. Wu prepared for the training session with some warm-ups, as he would have back home. They ate some more of the food they had brought with them, and finally the sun set and nearly full moon rose in the sky.

Whoosh! Nineko silently dropped from the tree house and landed between the boys.

"It is time to begin training," she said.

"Can you teach us how to do that? What you just did?" Garmadon asked eagerly.

"And back in that foggy forest, you jumped up so high," Wu added. "I'd love to learn that, too."

Nineko's long gray tail emerged from her kimono. The tip of it pointed at them.

"Cats have strong hind legs that power their jumps, and tails that help them keep balance," she explained.

"You two do not have those things. But you can learn. Follow me."

Without warning, she leapt straight into the air and landed on the deck of the tree house.

"How are we . . . ? You haven't taught us how to do that yet!" Garmadon yelled up.

"Use the ladder," she replied.

Both boys scrambled up the ladder. Nineko pointed to a thick green twisted vine that extended from the deck to a tree in the distance.

"Balance," she said. She stepped on the vine and glided across it with swift, sure steps until she reached the tree on the other side.

"I'll go first!" Garmadon offered.

He placed one foot on the vine and then stretched out both arms at his sides. He slowly took one step after another.

"Hey, that's pretty good," Wu said.

"I do this on the old stone wall at home," Garmadon said. "It's not that hard. You just need to concen—Whoa!"

Garmadon slipped and fell off the vine. He grabbed on with one hand to stop his fall. Then he tried to pull himself up.

"It's slippery!" he complained. "This vine is covered with lake slime."

"Hold on!" Wu cried.

He stepped out onto the vine and slowly made his way across, trying to reach his brother. But just before he reached him, he lost his footing. He tumbled off the vine, knocking into Garmadon and taking him down with him.

Splat! They landed in sticky, squishy mud.

"I could have gotten back on the vine!" Garmadon yelled. "Now look at us!"

"I was just trying to help," Wu replied.

Nineko jumped down from the tree, landing smoothly beside them.

"You do not have tails," she said. "So you must bring balance to your body. Garmadon, I can see you feel it. You did very well by using your outstretched arms. Next time, focus your energy in the bottom of your spine as you walk."

Then Nineko turned to Wu. "You will need to try harder. Use your staff to help you. Now let me see you both again."

Whoosh!

She ascended back up to the tree.

The boys climbed the ladder and tried again.

Splat! Splat! Splat! Splat!

They ended up in the mud again and again and again . . . until Garmadon finally made it across.

Determined not to fail, Wu concentrated as hard as he could . . . and he made it, too.

Wu leaned back against the tree trunk. "Finally!"

"Your training is hardly final," Nineko said. "But it is a good beginning."

"Can you teach us how to leap straight into the air, like you do? And land silently on your feet when you jump down?" Garmadon asked.

"I have abilities that you do not," Nineko replied. "But you can use your Spinjitzu to do the same. Watch closely as I jump."

She leapt off the branch and smoothly somersaulted in midair so that she landed evenly on her feet when she hit the rough ground.

"Use your Spinjitzu when you jump!" she said.

Wu understood. "I will go first this time," he said. He closed his eyes.

"Ninjaaa-go!" he cried as he launched himself off the branch. As he plummeted, he created a swirling Spinjitzu tornado. When he hit the ground, he kept spinning.

Wham! He slammed into a big tree trunk and fell backward.

"That was the right idea," Nineko called down. "You just need more control."

Garmadon tried next and had the same result, spinning wildly out off balance as he landed. The brothers tried again and again and again until the sun rose.

Nineko yawned. "Time for another nap," she said. "We will continue tonight."

Exhausted and covered in mud, Wu and Garmadon unrolled their mats on the deck of the tree house and slept. When they woke up, they washed their clothes in some clear water from a well. That night, the training began all over again.

"As you use your Spinjitzu to jump down, you may also use it to jump up," Nineko instructed. "Begin to spin before you launch off the ground."

She demonstrated, quickly twirling and then rocketing straight up into the air, landing on a tree branch high above.

"That looks easy!" Garmadon said. He spun and launched—but he couldn't even get half as high as Nineko.

"Let me try," Wu said, and the same thing happened to him.

Nineko jumped down. "It's all in the timing," she said. "The more you spin, the higher you'll be able to jump. But you'll also risk going out of control. It will take practice."

After their night of training, the boys tried to get more information out of Nineko.

"How did you meet our father?"

"How long did you train with him for?"

"Why did you leave the monastery?"

For several nights, she only twitched her ears and said nothing. On the fifth night, she finally gave in.

"I was an orphan girl," she began as they drank their tea by candlelight in the tree house. "Hungry and alone, I stole to feed myself and stay alive. Your father caught me stealing eggs from his henhouse. But instead of punishing me, he offered to train me."

The brothers looked at each other.

"That was a pretty generous thing for Father to do," Wu remarked.

"Yeah, maybe he has a heart after all," Garmadon said.

Nineko's eyes flickered and she said no more.

They continued to train each night until the sun came up. They went to bed muddy and exhausted, woke up and got clean, and then spent another night training.

Garmadon was eager to please Nineko.

"Nineko, look! Look!" he would cry as he walked across the vine. She would shake her head.

"Fail," she would say. "The goal of a ninja is to be invisible, not to be seen."

Wu persisted in trying to get Nineko to say more about her past.

"It's weird that she won't just tell us her story," he said to Garmadon one morning as they fetched fresh water from the well.

"It's not weird. She's just mysterious," Garmadon said. "All powerful ninja are mysterious, right? I'm just happy that she's teaching us her Catjitzu skills."

"I guess," Wu said, but he still wasn't satisfied. The next morning, he pressed Nineko again.

"Did you leave my father before or after you . . . became like you are now?" he asked one morning, when training was done.

Nineko's eyes narrowed. "I see there is no satisfying your curiosity," she said. "I will answer your question— after you master Catjitzu."

"Awwwww!" Wu groaned, but it pressed both him and his brother to work harder. Day after day they walked the vine, practiced jumping, and got covered in mud. Finally, when Wu thought they might never get it, something kicked in.

Both Wu and Garmadon walked across the twisted vine gracefully with perfect balance. They leapt from the tree house deck and landed silently on their feet on the muddy ground. They jumped effortlessly from the bottom of the tree and landed just beneath Nineko.

"Well done," she said.

"NOW you can tell us about training with our father," Wu said.

Garmadon rolled his eyes. "Sheesh, Wu—couldn't you even wait a minute?"

"I will keep my promise," Nineko said. "I trained with your father for several years. Then one day, shortly after my eighteenth birthday, one of his katanas went missing. Your father accused me of stealing it. I had not, but there was no way to convince him. I realized then that he would always see me as the young thief that he had rescued. So I continued training on my own."

"I—I'm sorry," Wu stammered, and Nineko jumped to the tree house without another word.

Garmadon punched him in the arm. "Nice job, Wu," he said. "She obviously didn't want to tell us because it's such a painful story. And you made her tell it."

"How was I supposed to know?" Wu asked. "Still . . . I mean, that sounds like something Father would do, but . . ."

"But what, Wu?" Garmadon said sternly. "Father's right. You're too curious for your own good sometimes. Come on, let's fetch some water for Nineko."

The boys collected a bucket of water and brought it up to the tree house. Nineko was staring out the window. She turned when they arrived.

"Now it is time for you to keep your promise," she said. "When first light breaks, you may begin your mission for me."

"Where are we going?" Wu asked.

"Back to the tall mountain where you encountered the jewel thieves," Nineko replied. "You will have to get past them, but I know a way that is not guarded. The Cat-Eye Jewel is on the very top of the mountain. You will need to use all your skills to reach it. Then you must bring it back to me."

"We'll get it for you, Nineko!" Garmadon promised. Then he yawned. "The sun will be up soon. Can't we wait until the afternoon?"

"I have waited long enough," Nineko said coldly, and she entered her house.

There she goes again being mysterious, Wu thought. *Why won't she tell us more about this Cat-Eye Jewel?*

But there was no point in pressing it. She had kept her end of the bargain by training them, and they owed it to her.

You had a bargain with Aspheera, too, a little voice in his head reminded him. *And that ended in a lot of trouble. Still, a deal is a deal. . . .*

The brothers slept for a short time and woke at first light to get ready for the mission. Nineko served them tea and a light breakfast, and then they followed her to the shore of the lake.

"Take the boat," she instructed, "and head west. There is a stream that feeds into the lake from a cavern beneath the mountain. Take the stream into the cavern. Then pass through the cavern and begin your climb. You should not encounter any of the thieves. When you get the jewel, bring it back to me."

"We won't fail you!" Garmadon assured her.

"I hope you won't," Nineko said. Then she leapt up, leaving them on the shore.

Wu and Garmadon climbed into the boat and began to row, staring at the murky surface of the green lake. After an hour they came to the stream that Nineko had mentioned. They rowed the boat toward

the mouth of the stream, getting close to the shore for the first time.

Wu noticed a rustling in a clump of reeds near where the lake and the stream met. He put a finger to his lips and motioned with his head to his brother. Garmadon followed his gaze and saw it, too.

The boys stopped rowing. Then they stood up, jumped from the boat onto the shore, and tackled the figure in the reeds. It was one of the green warriors!

Wu pinned the warrior to the ground with his staff. Garmadon pulled off the man's hood.

"You're not a cat ninja!' Garmadon exclaimed.

"Why would I be a cat ninja?" the warrior asked.

"Well, those ears kind of scream 'cat,'" Wu remarked.

"I'm obviously not a cat," the man replied.

Garmadon nodded. "We got that. But why are you following us? And are there others with you?"

"It's just me," the warrior said. "I've been watching you for several days. You need to listen to me. *I* am not your enemy. *Nineko* is!"

Chapter 6
Ninja or Sorceress?

The brothers gasped.

"He's lying to save himself," Garmadon said. "I'm going to check the perimeter."

"I don't need to lie to do that," the warrior said. "I'm a trained warrior. If I wanted to fight you, I'd be doing it right now."

"We'll see about that," Garmadon growled, and he darted off, scouting for other fighters in green, while Wu kept his staff pressed firmly on the warrior's chest.

Garmadon returned. "He's alone. He's telling the truth about that at least."

"I have no reason to lie to you kids!" the warrior countered. "I'm sure Nineko told you that we are

thieves. That we stole the Cat-Eye Jewel from her. But that's not the case. Let me tell you my story."

Wu slowly removed his staff.

"Talk," he said.

The man in green sat up. "My name is Dillon, and I am a member of the Ancient Order of Felis. It is our sacred duty to guard the Cat-Eye Jewel."

"After you stole it from Nineko?" Garmadon asked.

"It was never hers to steal," Dillon replied. "The Ancient Order of Felis has been guarding the Cat-Eye

Jewel for centuries, long before she was born. The stone is what gives each cat nine lives."

"I thought that was just a tale," Wu said.

Dillon replied. "It has been true ever since the stone was created. Because the life of a cat is precious, and often dangerous, the stone protects them by giving each one eight extra lives. However, any cat who harvests the power of the stone will steal *all* of the lives it holds and become immortal. That is why we guard it so carefully. The mountain is magically protected so that no cat can climb it."

"That is why Nineko asked us to retrieve the jewel for her," Wu said.

"You mean *steal* the jewel," Dillon said. "That's what she was trying to do when we stopped her. She used dark sorcery to transform herself into a cat so she could steal the stone and use its powers, but we foiled her plan."

"Wait, what do you mean, sorcery?" Garmadon asked. "Do you mean magic? She's a ninja, not some kind of witch."

"I'm sure she showed you only what she wanted you to see," Dillon replied.

Wu remembered Nineko's mysterious refusal to answer most questions.

Is that what she was hiding? he thought.

"The Order of Felis knows her as an evil sorceress, one who committed terrible acts in her pursuit of immortality," he said. "That is why she wants the Cat-Eye Jewel. She wants to steal all the lives for herself."

Garmadon frowned. "You want us to believe that Nineko turned herself into a cat lady on purpose?"

Dillon nodded. "That is what happened," he said. "If you don't believe me, come with me to the Temple of Felis. Our leader will give you the proof you need."

Garmadon scowled at Wu. "You don't think he's telling the truth, do you? He's just making up a story so we won't help Nineko take back what's rightfully hers."

"I don't know," Wu replied slowly. "Nineko said the green warriors were thieves. But if they wanted to profit from the stone, why are they protecting it? Why not sell it? Or use whatever powers it has for themselves?"

He looked at Dillon. "I want to hear more. Take us to your leader."

"No way!" Garmadon said. "We need to tie this guy up and do what Nineko asked us to do."

The brothers stared at each other fiercely.

"I think we should go talk to the other guardians," Wu said. "See if the story checks out."

"You mean walk into a trap?" Garmadon asked.

"We can handle ourselves," Wu said. "If Nineko really is evil, then I don't want to help her."

"She trained us in Catjitzu! She saved us twice!" Garmadon cried. "I can't believe you're being serious right now, Wu. Let's do what we came to do. We must keep our promise to Nineko."

Wu shook his head. "I can't, Garmadon. Not until I get more information."

Garmadon turned and walked toward the shore.

"Where are you going?" Wu asked.

"Back to Nineko. I trust her. Are you coming with me?" Garmadon asked.

"No!" Wu replied. "How can you trust her after what we've heard?"

"Never mind. I don't need you," Garmadon snapped. "I'm going to figure out how to keep our promise." He jumped into the boat and rowed away.

Wu had never seen Garmadon act like this. He watched his brother disappear across the lake. *Will I ever see him again?* he thought.

Chapter 7
The Search for Immortality

Garmadon hated the idea of going back to Nineko without the jewel. He thought about climbing the mountain himself, but now the thieves—or the guardians, *if* their story was true—would be looking for him. He wasn't sure if he could take them on all by himself. He didn't want to admit it, but he needed Wu.

He's so stubborn! Garmadon thought. *We had one simple thing to do, and Wu had to go mess it up. He'd rather believe the word of a stranger—a thief!—than agree with his own brother.*

Another little voice in the back of Garmadon's head told him that Wu might be right. Dillon's story could be true, and if that were the case, it would be a bad thing for Nineko to get the jewel. *Very bad.* But he didn't want Wu to be right. Something inside him pulled him toward Nineko. He couldn't really explain it, but he felt that they had a connection somehow. And he wanted to hear what she had to say.

He rowed back across the lake and leapt to the deck of the tree house. He found Nineko inside, meditating. As soon as he stepped into the tree house, she opened an eye.

"You have failed," she said.

"Not exactly," Garmadon said. "Wu and I found a scout following us. He told us that he belonged to an ancient order of guards protecting the Cat-Eye Jewel. He says the stone was never yours to begin with. That you only want to steal it to become immortal and that you are a sorceress who did terrible things in your quest for immortality. Wu believed him, but I didn't."

Nineko stood up. "I knew you were different from your brother, Garmadon," she said. "You were wise to come to me."

She placed a tea kettle on the stove. Then she took a jar from her shelf and spooned some of the contents into two cups.

"I will make tea and we will talk," she said. They sat across from each other on the floor. Both were silent until the tea was ready.

Nineko sipped her tea. Her mesmerizing yellow eyes stared at Garmadon.

"What the guard told you is mostly true," she said.

Garmadon's mouth dropped open. "You mean you are a . . ."

"A sorceress," she said calmly. "But now I can tell you my whole story, Garmadon. I know that you, more than anyone else, will understand."

She trusts me, Garmadon thought. And while a small part of his brain warned him to run, he stayed put. He wanted to hear her out.

"What your father did to me hurt, Garmadon," she began. "I had begun to think of him as the father I never had. And then he accused me of a terrible thing—something I did not do! I felt betrayed."

Garmadon nodded. "I . . . I know what it is to feel rejected by my father."

Nineko smiled. "Yes, I knew you would understand, Garmadon," she said. "Then you will understand what I did next. I vowed that one day, I would become better, stronger, and more powerful than the First Spinjitzu Master. I would return to him and show him that he should have believed in me."

That makes sense, Garmadon thought. *I probably would have done the same thing.*

"I tried to perfect Spinjitzu on my own," she told him. "But I knew it would not be enough to best your father and his ability to live for thousands of years. To beat him, I would have to become immortal."

"So you studied sorcery?" Garmadon asked.

"I did," she replied. "I sought out the teachings of dark magic. That is how I learned about the Cat-Eye Jewel."

Garmadon frowned. "The guardian said you did bad things—evil things—before you tried to steal the jewel."

Nineko waved her paw. "I did what had to be done," she said. "But nothing worked. The Cat-Eye Jewel was my last hope. I sacrificed my humanity to try to get it. And in my new form, I created the art of Catjitzu and practiced it for ten years. And yet the Order of Felis stopped me from achieving my goal. I need you to fulfill your promise to me, Garmadon. Steal the jewel and bring it to me."

"I . . . ," Garmadon began. He could practically hear his brother's voice in his head. *The guardian was right, Garmadon! She's a sorceress! Get out of there before something bad happens!*

Nineko raised an eyebrow. "You hesitate," she said, and sighed. "I did not want to have to do this. It would have been easier if you'd cooperated."

"Do what?" Garmadon asked.

Her long black hair snaked out from behind her head. The strands of hair looked alive as they reached for Garmadon.

Dark magic, Garmadon thought, and he watched, transfixed, as the rippling black strands continued toward him.

"What . . . what's happening?" he asked.

The brave ninja tried to move, but he was frozen to the spot.

"Don't worry, Garmadon," Nineko said, her dark eyes sparkling hypnotically as her captive grew quiet. "This won't hurt a bit!"

Chapter 8
The Temple of the Jewel Guardians

For a split second, Wu had thought about jumping into the boat with his brother. If Nineko was a sorceress, he was only heading for trouble. But he stopped himself.

Let him go, Wu thought. *He won't listen to reason. Let him find out for himself.*

He turned to Dillon. "What now?"

"In recent months, we have seen Nineko working strange magic in the rain," the scout replied. "She is up to something. And with your brother's help, she may finally succeed in stealing the jewel."

"He won't help her if he knows she's evil," Wu says. "Once he learns the truth, he'll come back here."

Dillon shook his head. "She has ways of making others do her bidding. Come with me to the Temple of the Jewel Guardians. We must warn the others."

Wu glanced back at the lake. "I'll go with you," he said. "But you're wrong about Garmadon."

Dillon didn't argue. He remained silent as he led Wu away from the mountain and through the woods. After a short hike, the woods opened into a clearing with a tall tower in the center.

Wu gazed up at the structure. He had never seen anything like it. The tower was seven stories tall, with a large round opening at each level. Platforms jutted out at different heights, and Wu could see the green-clad guardians jumping from one platform to the next.

"This is where we live and train," Dillon explained. "Our mission is to guard the jewel."

As they got closer, Wu saw hundreds of actual cats all around the building—white cats, orange cats, black

cats, gray cats, and cats with a patchwork of fur in all the colors. Some cats merrily tumbled around on the grass in front of the tower or chased each other around it. Others napped in the sunlight. More cats climbed up the tower, jumping from platform to platform.

"All cats are welcome here," Dillon told Wu. "Many strays have made our temple their home."

Wu sniffed the air and made a wry face. "What's that smell?"

"The whole first floor is full of sand for our guests, so they can—well, you know," Dillon said. "Follow me! Humans enter on the second floor."

Dillon jumped from platform to platform until he reached the entrance. Wu followed him up and inside.

"This is our training room," Dillon said.

Dozens of guardians in green hoods were training in an obstacle course that reminded Wu of his father's training room. Some raced across the room, jumping

over barrels. Others swung on ropes hanging from the ceiling. Two guardians sparred with long spears.

"This is some serious training," Wu remarked.

Dillon nodded. "We take our duties very seriously."

As they spoke, one of the guards ran toward them. She lowered her green hood and red hair cascaded down her shoulders.

"Dillon, what have you learned?" she asked. "And where is the other ninja?"

"This is Wu, Adara," Dillon answered. "His brother, Garmadon, has gone back to Nineko."

Adara frowned. "Then we must prepare for another attack," she said. "Before these ninja arrived, Nineko was working on some new magic."

"Summoning monsters again?" Dillon asked.

Adara shook her head. "I'm not sure. All we know is that it has something to do with her umbrella."

"What did you mean about Nineko summoning monsters?" Wu asked, remembering the beast from the forest. "By any chance, do they look like tiger-lizard-bears? And have terrible breath, too?"

"She uses magic to summon monsters from remote parts of the island—monsters that none of us have ever seen before," Dillon explained. "She has summoned some horrible creatures in her quest to steal the jewel. She made them fight us. But some wouldn't obey her, and now they roam free in the woods and hunt unwary travelers. . . ."

Wu frowned. "I still can't believe that Nineko is an evil sorceress," he said. "She seems so normal—except for the whole half-cat thing."

"I will bring you to our leader, as I promised," Dillon told him.

Adara nodded. "I will organize a unit to guard the perimeter of the mountain," she said. "Meet me there."

"We will," Dillon promised, and she hurried away. He motioned to Wu. "Come on. Library's on the fourth level."

They climbed up ladders until they reached the fourth floor. Paintings of cats covered the walls, and shelves of books filled the room. In the center, a woman with white hair and a wrinkled face sat cross-legged on a large pillow with her eyes closed. On a small table in front of her, fragrant incense burned.

Dillon and Wu approached her, and Dillon bowed.

"Komala, this is one of the ninja I told you about," he said.

The leader of the guardians opened an eye. "Please sit," she said as she nodded to Wu.

"Dillon said you could prove to me that Nineko is a sorceress," Wu said, sitting on the floor in front of her.

"I can," Komala said. "Look into the smoke, ninja."

She motioned toward the curl of smoke coming from the incense. Wu watched it, confused, but then images began to appear inside it.

"I was a little girl when Nineko came to my village," she said, and an image of Komala as a young girl appeared in the smoke. "She cast a spell on our crops—she tried to become immortal by draining the life from them."

The image changed to a woman with long black hair in a kimono that looked very much like Nineko.

She stood in a wheat field with her arms outstretched. Her hair floated behind her as waves of energy flowed from the plants into her fingertips. The crops grew black and withered.

"Nineko's spell failed and she wasn't able to take the life force from our crops. But our crops did die and my village nearly starved," Komala said.

Wu nodded. "Dillon was right. That is evil."

"And that is not all she has done," Komala continued. "She casts spells that summon horrible monsters. . . ."

"I know," Wu said. "We met one of them."

"Then you understand," Komala said. "After what I witnessed, I devoted my life to the study of good magic so I could stop evil sorcerers like Nineko. The Order of Felis sought me out to help protect the Cat-Eye Jewel, and I agreed. And when Nineko showed up to steal it, I wasn't surprised. Her thirst for immortality was so strong that I knew she would stop at nothing to use the jewel's powers for herself."

More images appeared in the smoke. First Nineko, in her human form, transforming into a cat in front of the Cat Eye-Jewel so she could take possession of it.

Then Komala appeared, sending Nineko tumbling with a magical blast.

"I placed a spell on the Cat-Eye Jewel so that no human could steal its lives, but Nineko was clever. She transformed into a cat so she could obtain its power," Komala continued. "We stopped her just in time, and then I put many spells on the mountain so no cats can climb it. They are welcome in the temple, but not on the mountain."

"She transformed herself into a cat for nothing," Wu said.

"Not nothing," Komala replied. "She did gain the nine lives of a cat. But she has probably lost several of them already, which is why she is so desperate to get the jewel."

Komala paused for a moment, then said, "Nineko has tried to send humans to fetch the jewel for her before, but none could get past our guards. Even her monsters could not defeat them. She was very lucky

to have two Spinjitzu ninja fall into her clutches. And where is the other?"

"He returned to Nineko," Wu said, standing up. "And he is in danger!"

"We must go to the mountain," Dillon said. "We can intercept them there."

"Yes, I can sense that she is near," Komala said. "Go, quickly!"

Wu and Dillon climbed down the tower and hurried toward the mountain. When they reached the base, they saw three lines of guardians there. Adara approached them.

"Our scout just returned from the lake," she said. "Nineko and Garmadon are on their way."

Wu looked at all the guardians. "There are two of them against all of us, right? That shouldn't be a problem. I'll get to Garmadon and tell him that Nineko is bad news. If I can talk some sense into him, this will all be over."

At that moment, a green mist crept toward the mountain, rolling low on the ground. As the mist

reached Wu and the guardians, Nineko and Garmadon emerged from it.

"Garmadon!" Wu yelled. "Nineko is a sorceress! You can't trust her!"

Nineko smiled, and Garmadon stared ahead, blankly.

"Garmadon!" Wu cried again, and then he noticed something—his brother's eyes glowed with a strange green light.

Dillon tugged on his sleeve. "She is controlling him with magic," he said. "We can help him, but we must defeat her first."

Wu held his staff in front of him and stepped forward.

"Release my brother, Nineko!" he demanded. "You will never be able to defeat all of us. Give up now!"

Nineko held up her umbrella. "You are correct. Your brother and I cannot defeat all of you alone," she said. "But we are not alone."

She opened the umbrella. Suddenly, green clouds began to form in the sky. A wind whipped through the foothills.

"What new sorcery is this?" Adara asked.

Big, green raindrops began to splash onto the ground. Then the water quickly began to take shape. One by one, cat-shaped warriors made of rain sprang up from the ground.

Wu gasped. "It's an army of rain cats!"

"Those aren't just rain cats," Dillon said. "It looks like the sorceress has used her umbrella to awaken the legendary Warriors of Felis!"

"And that's not good, is it?" Wu asked.

"No," Dillion replied. "No, it is not."

Chapter 9
Get the Jewel!

The cat warriors glowed with green energy. They were larger than house cats, and they all had sleek bodies, rippled muscles, and extra-sharp teeth.

"Whoa," Wu said. "Is Nineko going to use them to steal the jewel?"

"No cats can touch it, not even cat warriors made of rain," Dillon reminded him. "She's using them to battle us so your brother can steal the jewel."

"Attack!" Nineko yelled.

Wu knew he had to reach Garmadon. *I have to save him from Nineko's sorcery somehow,* he thought.

"Ninjaaa-go!" he cried as he launched into a twirling Spinjitzu tornado. He plowed into a crowd of the cat warriors, expecting them to burst into water droplets, but they felt impossibly solid! Even so, he became drenched with water after attacking them.

"They're made of rain, but they're also solid!" Wu cried. "How are we supposed to defeat them?"

He knocked a few of them aside, but more began to circle him at high speed. Wu tried to spin through them. They were creating so much energy that he kept getting pushed back.

He stopped spinning. *Think, Wu!* The cats still raced around him. The air was filled with cries of cats screeching and the confused battle cries of the jewel guardians.

"We can't fight them—they're cats!"

"They're not *actual* cats. They're magic!"

"We must battle them to protect the jewel."

And then he heard Nineko. "Garmadon, fetch me the jewel!"

Wu began to spin again. This time, he performed Catjitzu, launching himself high above the circle of cats.

At least something good came out of meeting Nineko! he thought.

He landed in front of Garmadon.

"Nineko has you under some kind of spell, brother!" Wu said. "Come with me back to the temple of the jewel guardians. We'll find some way to help you."

Garmadon stared blankly at Wu through the eerie green light that filled his eyes.

"I must get the Cat-Eye Jewel," he said. His voice sounded weirdly flat.

Wu grabbed him by the shoulders and shook him. "Snap out of it, Garmadon!"

Garmadon picked up Wu and flipped him backward. Then he ran toward the mountain. Wu scrambled to his feet and took off after him.

As he ran, the jewel guardians fought off the cat warriors. Three cat warriors had Dillon cornered in a tree. Adara delivered a sideways kick to one of the cats, sending it flying.

I'm the only one who can stop Garmadon, Wu thought, and he ran even faster. He had to get to the bottom of the mountain before his brother did.

At first glance, the mountain seemed impossible to climb. Then Wu noticed narrow wedges of rock sticking out of it, staggered from the bottom all the way to the top.

Just like the temple, Wu thought. *It's why Nineko taught us Catjitzu! We can't reach the top without it.*

When Garmadon got to the base of the mountain, he realized that, too, and he began to spin. Then he

rocketed straight up into the air and landed on the first rock platform.

"Garmadon! Stop!" Wu yelled, and he jumped up and landed on another empty platform.

Zoom! Zoom! Zoom! The two boys sprang from rocky ledge to rocky ledge, using what Nineko had taught them to ascend the mountain.

Garmadon reached the top of the mountain a few seconds before Wu. Two green-clad guardians waited

for them there, holding long spears. They looked surprised to see the ninja.

"My brother is under a spell!" Wu called out. "Don't let him get the jewel. But don't hurt him!"

"We must guard the jewel at all costs!" one of the guardians cried, and they charged at Garmadon with their spears.

Wu hesitated. *If I battle the guards, Garmadon gets the jewel. But I can't let them hurt my brother!*

Just then, Garmadon jumped into the air between the two guards.

Whack! Whack! He delivered a kick to each guard, sending them sprawling. He ran off, and Wu followed.

The biggest jewel Wu and Garmadon had ever seen was perched on the mountain's peak. A streak of black through the center made it look just like the eye of a cat. It was the jewel Komala had shown to Wu in the smoke.

"Mine!" Garmadon cried, and he reached for the jewel.

"Not so fast!" Wu cried, reaching for it, too.

The brothers grappled for control of the prize. Wu felt the rocks underneath his feet crumble. Garmadon

grabbed for the jewel, and the two boys, along with the jewel, tumbled off the mountain peak. They plummeted to the ground below. Wu knew there was only one way to land safely.

"Garmadon, spin!" Wu yelled as he began spinning like a tornado.

Garmadon hesitated, but his sense of self-preservation kicked in, and he launched into a Spinjitzu tornado.

Wu and Garmadon hit the ground. The boys landed on their feet and stopped spinning, kicking up

dust behind them. The jewel crashed to the ground a split second later, and both boys leapt to claim it.

They wrestled for the jewel, rolling around across the rocks. Then the tangle of brothers broke up and they both somersaulted in different directions.

Wu looked down at the Cat-Eye Jewel in his arms.

I got it! he thought.

"Give that to ME!" Garmadon raged. The magical green glow in his eyes now burned like a flame.

Dillon and Adara raced over. "We've got this, Wu. You get the jewel back to the top of the mountain, and we'll stop your brother!" Dillon yelled.

He lunged at Garmadon and flipped him onto his back. Adara jumped up and kicked Garmadon as he tried to get up.

Wu raced toward the mountain path.

Whoosh!

Nineko landed in front of him, her black hair streaming behind her like snakes. She held her umbrella in front of her like a fighting staff, ready to attack.

"There is nowhere to run, Wu," she said. "Give me the jewel, and I will remove the magical hold I have on your brother."

"I don't trust you," Wu said. "Release Garmadon first. Then you can have the jewel."

"Enough games!" Nineko hissed, and her hair reached out and tried to grab Wu.

He backflipped to get away and then turned and ran. He scanned to see if there were any jewel guardians nearby that he could pass the jewel to—but they were all busy battling the relentless cat warriors. He couldn't see Dillon, Adara, or Garmadon.

He went to the edge of the same ravine he and his brother had fallen into before and skidded to a stop. Nineko advanced on him.

"No bargaining," she said. "Give me the jewel!"

"I must get the jewel!" His brother's eerie voice sounded behind Wu.

Garmadon leapt out of nowhere and tackled Wu. The two boys nearly tumbled over the edge again.

"Brother, stop!" Wu begged as they wrestled for the jewel once more. "We're going to fall!"

Garmadon didn't listen. He kicked Wu in the knees, and the jewel fell out of his hands. Nineko leapt toward them and picked up the jewel with the rippling strands of her hair.

"It's mine!" she said, her yellow eyes glittering. "It's finally mine!"

"I MUST GET THE JEWEL!" Garmadon said.

"Garmadon, no!" the sorceress said. "When I commanded you to get the jewel, it was so you would give it to *me*."

"THE JEWEL!" Garmadon repeated, and Wu laughed.

"You're not very good at casting spells, are you?" he said.

Garmadon tackled Nineko, and she tumbled onto her back. The jewel flew from her grasp and Wu dove for it. His heart was pounding as the jewel landed in his arms.

"It's mine!" Nineko yelled. As she jumped up, she slipped on the uneven rocks at the edge of the ravine.

"Nineko!" Wu cried.

He rushed toward her, but he was a split second too late.

Arms flailing as she fell backward, Nineko plunged over the edge. Wu held his breath as he peered into the ravine.

Had Nineko managed to grab hold of a rock?

But he saw nothing. Then he heard his brother's voice behind him.

"I MUST GET THE JEWEL!" Garmadon cried, and he lunged at Wu.

Chapter 10
The Spell Is Broken

Wu gasped and raced away from the edge of the ravine with Garmadon at his heels. A squadron of rain cats approached from the other side, surrounding Wu.

Wu clutched the Cat-Eye Jewel to his chest. "Snap out of it, Garmadon!" he pleaded. "Nineko's evil, and she just proved it! And now she's gone. You don't have to obey her anymore."

But Garmadon was still under the spell. "The jewel," he said, and he launched into a Spinjitzu tornado. The rain cats pounced. Wu spun in a circle, sizing up the danger from all dimensions.

Looks like I'm doomed! he thought. *But at least I'll go out fighting like a true ninja!*

But before he could yell "Ninjago!" the rain cats began to dissolve into clouds of mist.

Poof! Poof! Poof!

A woman slowly walked through the mist, supported by a cane.

"Komala!" Wu cried.

She pointed at the spinning Garmadon, and white light streamed from her fingertip. He slowed down and then stood still. The green glow disappeared from Garmadon's eyes and a confused look crossed his face.

"What happened?" he asked. "I was just in Nineko's house. Why am I here?"

"Nineko had you under a spell," Komala told him. "I'm not much of a fighter these days, but once I saw those rain cats, I knew my magic could help."

"Thank you!" Wu said, and he ran to Garmadon and hugged him. "It's good to have you back!"

Dillon and Adara walked up to the brothers.

"Yes. Nineko is gone and her magic is broken—for now," Dillon said.

The other jewel guardians gathered around, some limping, others battered from their battles.

"Nineko must have used magic to make Garmadon want to get the jewel no matter what," Wu said. He gazed toward the ravine. "I guess it backfired on her. The spell she cast on my brother led to her own undoing."

"Nineko will return," Komala added. "She still has some lives left. And as the sworn guardians of the Order of Felis, we must continue to protect the Cat-Eye Jewel."

"Forever Felis!" the cat guardians cheered.

Wu held out the Cat-Eye Jewel. "This belongs to you, then," he said.

"Um, about that," Dillon said. "Would you guys mind taking it back to the top of the mountain?

I mean, we could do it, but it's a long climb, and you did it really fast with your ninja powers, and . . ."

Garmadon looked up at the mountain. "We climbed up there?"

Wu nodded. "Yup."

Garmadon grabbed the jewel from Wu and grinned. "First one to the top wins!"

Garmadon took off, and Wu smiled. It was good to see his brother back to his old self.

Then he raced after Garmadon. "I'm right behind you, brother!"

Epilogue

Sunlight shone through the window of Master Wu's room. The rain had gone.

"Well, that was a really *paw*-some story, Master Wu," Jay joked.

"I'm glad Nineko didn't get the Cat-Eye Jewel," Lloyd said. "Can you imagine a villain like that with the power of immortality? That would be bad news."

"Wait, how did you end up with the umbrella?" Cole asked.

"Years later, Dillon and Adara brought it to me," Master Wu replied. "They found the umbrella in the ravine, but they never found Nineko. Although, they were certain that she would return someday. I have

kept the umbrella ever since. It reminds me of how close I came to losing my brother forever."

Kai jumped up. "Now that it's nice out, let's get back to training!"

"Yes," Zane agreed. "We have only two hours, seventeen minutes, and five point four seconds of daylight left. We should make the most of it."

Jay picked up the umbrella. "I know just how we should train. Rain cats!"

He ran outside, and the others followed. Master Wu shook his head.

"Jay, remember what my father told us," he warned. "Curiosity killed the cat."

Jay didn't listen. "Come on, rain cats! Let's see how *furr*-ocious you are!"

He opened the umbrella—and a flood of water poured from the umbrella canopy and drenched him.

Master Wu grinned.

"You must be a true sorceress to summon rain cats," he said. "As you can see, anyone else who uses the umbrella just gets wet."

"Yeah, I figured that out," Jay said with a sigh.

Nya turned to Master Wu. "You never told us what happened to you and Garmadon. Did you reach the northern ocean? Did you find the plant your father asked you to get?"

"Our journey took a long time, and there are more stories to tell," Master Wu said. "But those are stories for another day."

He gazed up at the clouds as the memories washed over him.

Glossary

Adara

A skilled warrior and member of the Ancient Order of Felis (also known as the Jewel Guardians), a mysterious organization protecting the powerful Cat-Eye Jewel for many centuries.

Aspheera

A treacherous Serpentine sorceress who in her younger days encountered Wu and Garmadon. She set the brothers free from the Serpentine prison, on the condition they would teach her Spinjitzu. Wu agreed, but Aspheera used her new skill to overthrow the Serpentine king and invade Ninjago. The brothers stole the scrolls of Forbidden Spinjitzu from their father to gain the power necessary to stop Aspheera.

Cat-Eye Jewel

A legendary magical jewel that gives cats nine lives. According to renowned sorcerers, any cat that harvests the power of the stone will possess all of the lives it holds and become immortal.

Cole

Cole is a member of Master Wu's ninja team. As the Earth Ninja, he wields the elemental power of Earth and supports his friends with his confidence and great physical strength.

Dillon

A brave warrior and member of the Ancient Order of Felis, Dillon is also one of the best scouts among the Jewel Guardians.

First Spinjitzu Master

The father of Wu and Garmadon, and the powerful creator of Spinjitzu and the entire world of Ninjago. The First Spinjitzu Master trained his sons in the art of Spinjitzu, hoping that one day they would become his successors, protecting the world he had created against the forces of darkness.

Garmadon

Wu's older brother and a son of the First Spinjitzu Master. Bitten by a vile snake as a child, Garmadon gradually filled with evil to become Lord Garmadon, the greatest villain in the world of Ninjago.

Gi

A type of clothing traditionally worn by ninja.

Jay

The Lightning Ninja is quick-witted, talks fast, and often acts before he thinks. Without Jay's sense of humor, the ninja team would be in a much worse mood.

Kai

Kai is the Fire Ninja. With his fierce temper, bravery, and strong sense of justice, he'll stop at nothing if he has put his mind to it.

Komala

The wise leader of the Jewel Guardians who had trained herself over many years in practicing good magic in order to protect her village and its people from evil sorcery.

Lloyd

Wise beyond his years, Lloyd is the Green Ninja and the leader of the ninja team. He is the son of Garmadon, the grandson of the First Spinjitzu Master, and Master Wu's nephew.

Nineko

A conniving sorceress whose only desire is to become immortal. To achieve her goal, Nineko needs the Cat-Eye Jewel. She believes she can get it with the help of Garmadon and Wu.

Nya

Kai's younger sister is the Water Ninja. She's a skilled warrior, inventor, and tech wiz. She's often the team's voice of reason and a steadfast support to her friends on every mission.

Scrolls of Forbidden Spinjitzu

Two scrolls of paper that contain the dark powers of Forbidden Spinjitzu. Although the maker of the scrolls, the First Spinjitzu Master, told his sons never to touch them, young Wu and Garmadon stole them to defeat a Serpentine sorceress called Aspheera.

Spinjitzu

A technique based on balance and rotation in which you tap into your elemental energy while turning quickly. Developed by the First Spinjitzu Master long before time had a name, Spinjitzu is more than a martial art: it's also a way of living. Mastering it is a lifelong journey.

Warriors of Felis

Cat warriors created from the rain with dark sorcery. To some, the Warriors of Felis are just a myth, but to those who have faced them, they're a dreadful force of evil.

Wu

Wu is the other son of the First Spinjitzu Master, and little brother to Garmadon. After many years of mastering the art of Spinjitzu and the ways of the ninja, Wu shares his knowledge with his students— Lloyd, Kai, Cole, Jay, Zane, and Nya—to train them as ninja protectors of the world of Ninjago.

Zane

Brave and caring Zane is the Titanium Ninja, wielding the elemental power of ice. He is a Nindroid (ninja robot), created to protect those who cannot protect themselves.